Paloma
WANTS TO BE LADY FREEDOM

WRITTEN BY

Rachel Campos-Duffy

ILLUSTRATED BY

Richard Johnson

Regnery Kids

Regnery Kids™ is a trademark of Salem Communications Holding Corporation;
Regnery® is a registered trademark of Salem Communications Holding Corporation

Cataloging-in-Publication data on file with the Library of Congress

ISBN 978-1-62157-970-0
e-book ISBN 978-1-62157-981-6
Published in the United States by
Regnery Kids, an imprint of
Regnery Publishing
A Division of Salem Media Group
300 New Jersey Ave NW
Washington, DC 20001
www.RegneryKids.com

Manufactured in the United States of America

10 9 8 7 6 5 4 3 2 1

Books are available in quantity for promotional or premium use.
For information on discounts and terms, please visit our website: www.Regnery.com.

To Paloma. Thank you for allowing me to see freedom through your eyes.

To my parents. You taught me to love America and appreciate the gift of citizenship.

To my children. You inspire me to keep fighting for freedom & the American Dream.

To Sean. Your service to our country fills my heart with pride.

A special thank you to my daughter, Lucia-Belen. Your insight & honesty were invaluable throughout this process. We're a great team!

"Freedom is never more than one generation away from extinction.
We didn't pass it to our children in the bloodstream. It must be fought for, protected,
and handed on for them to do the same."
—Ronald Reagan

5

6

Paloma was looking forward to Isabela's birthday party. Her whole class was going. But she was not. Her father had always dreamed of visiting Washington, D.C., the nation's Capitol. So Paloma was going, like it or not!

As her parents loaded the minivan, she couldn't help thinking about all the fun she'd be missing. "What's the big deal about becoming an American citizen anyway?" she grumbled under her breath while she watched over her baby sister, Margarita.

9

"The cherry blossom buds unfolded today!" her mother announced.
"Que suerte! Even the flowers are welcoming our familia," her father added,
hoping to cheer Paloma up. Still, all she could think about was the birthday party.

11

Her parents had a surprise. "We're going to see the monuments at night!"
She had never been allowed to stay up this late before.
As her Daddy took her picture on the steps in front of Abraham Lincoln,
Paloma thought about her friends breaking the birthday piñata.
The one thing that kept her from thinking about the party was the magnificent Capitol dome.
It was the prettiest building she had ever seen.

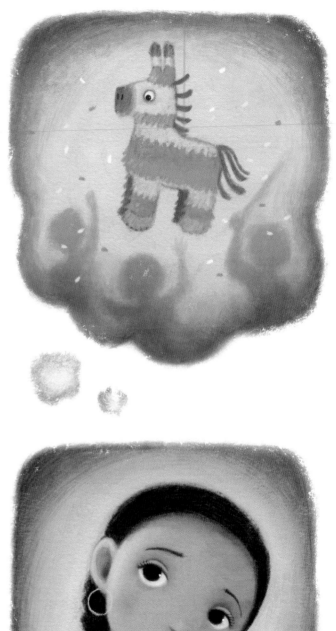

As they walked closer to the Capitol, she noticed something on top of it.

Paloma wondered what the beautiful Lady was doing up there.

She tugged her Daddy's hand.

"I want to go there and see the Lady!" she insisted.

"Mañana, Paloma. Tomorrow."

The Lady on top of the dome was even more splendid in daylight! She seemed to sparkle while watching over the whole city.
Paloma wanted to know all about her!

There were so many tourists inside the Capitol Visitor's Center. "No wonder they call it the 'People's House,'" thought Paloma. There she is! The lady on the top of the dome!
Paloma noticed her Daddy looking happy and proud—the way she remembered him the day he became a citizen.

19

Entering the Rotunda, a giant painting caught her attention.

"She's beautiful, isn't she?" interrupted a Capitol policeman.

"Yes!" said Paloma.

"Her name is Pocahontas," he informed her of the lady kneeling with the long brown hair.

"And there's another beautiful lady standing on this dome," Paloma told him, pointing to the high ceiling.

"That's right. Her name is Lady Freedom," he explained.
"President Abraham Lincoln built her during the Civil War."
"What does she do?" Paloma asked.
"She's a warrior, protecting freedom," the officer answered.
"My Daddy says he came to America for freedom," Paloma said.
"Many people do," replied the officer.
"I wanted to go to a birthday party, but we came here because
my Dad just became a citizen," Paloma explained.
"Well, the Capitol is the perfect place to celebrate citizenship."

Looking around, the officer asked, "Where are your parents?"

Paloma's eyes darted around the room, "They were just here," she said nervously.

"Don't worry, we'll find them," he said reassuringly. "I'm Officer Douglass. What's your name, little lady?"

"Paloma."

"Well, Paloma, did you know Lady Freedom is as tall as a giraffe?" he asked, trying to calm her.

Through quivering lips she said, "That's tall. I'm the smallest in my class." In that moment she felt even smaller.

"Paloma, you can be brave like Lady Freedom," he reassured her.

"Did you notice she's facing east?"
Paloma shook her head.
"Well, that's because she's keeping her eye on old King George of England. She's up there guarding America against anyone who might want to take away our freedom," Officer Douglass explained.

25

"I like her helmet with the feathers,"
said Paloma.
"Those are Native American feathers,"
explained Officer Douglass.
"Like Pocahontas?" she asked.
"Yes, Native American, like Pocahontas,"
he smiled.
"Her feathers represent honor, strength,
and freedom," he continued. "You see, thanks
to the courage of Abraham Lincoln and the
abolitionists, in America, we're born free."
"Born free," repeated Paloma thoughtfully.

They wandered into an impressive room surrounded by statues.

"Even the floors are fancy!" exclaimed Paloma.

One of the statues caught her eye. It was somebody she learned about in school.

"I know her!" Paloma told Officer Douglass.

"Yes, Rosa Parks," said Officer Douglass.

Paloma remembered how Rosa refused to give up her seat on a bus.
She bravely said, "No!" because she wanted freedom for everyone.
"Rosa Parks is Lady Freedom too!" declared Paloma.
"She suuure was," agreed Officer Douglass.

"Paloma! Paloma!" her parents' frantic voices rang across the room.

"We've been looking all over for you!" her father cried.

"Daddy, this is where our freedoms are protected."

"Yes, I know, mi'ja. That's why I wanted you to come with us to Washington."

"Americans are born free!" she blurted out excitedly.

"That's right, Paloma! In America we're free to work hard and make our dreams come true."

"Can I be Lady Freedom too?" she asked her parents.

Before they could answer, Paloma fired off a bunch of questions.

"Will the shield be too heavy? If I get tired can I come down?

Can Margarita and Pablo come up and visit me?"

"Of course they can," smiled Officer Douglass as he placed a police badge sticker on her dress.

Paloma treasured the Lady Freedom keychain her mom bought her in the Capitol gift shop. On the car ride home, she never let it go.

As she watched the dome disappear, she thought about Lady Freedom, Abraham Lincoln, and Rosa Parks.

She knew she wanted to be just like them. She felt happy and proud to be an American.

"I'm glad we went to Washington, D.C., Daddy. I love America."

"Me too, mi'ja."

When her father opened the front door, Paloma ran straight to her bedroom where she hung Lady Freedom from the highest turret of her pink, plastic princess castle.

Looking up at her father she told him, "I want to be Lady Freedom, Daddy."

"You already are, Paloma. You already are."

About this book

Paloma Wants to Be Lady Freedom is based on the true story of a visit to the U.S. Capitol by Rachel's daughter Paloma. When her husband, Sean, was elected to Congress in 2010, neither of them had ever stepped foot inside the Capitol. As a mother, one of the greatest privileges of his election and his years of public service has been watching her children walk the halls of Congress at such young, formative ages. It was during her daughter Paloma's first trip to Washington, D.C., that she fell in love with the beauty and majesty of the building. Only five years old at the time, Paloma loved the magnificence of the building. She was especially fascinated by the bronze statue of Lady

Paloma, eight years old, returns often to the Capitol Rotunda.

Freedom at the top of the dome. To satisfy her curiosity, Rachel learned all she could about Lady Freedom. After hearing the statue's story, Paloma decided that she wanted to be Lady Freedom when she grew up (she even insisted on being Lady Freedom for Halloween that year!). It's this very sweet, personal story that inspired this book.

"My mother became a U.S. citizen when I was around the same age as the character in my book. At the time, I was too young to fully appreciate the powerful and emotional citizenship process my mother went through. Nonetheless, having an immigrant parent, as well as a father in the U.S. military, taught me to never take for granted that I am blessed to be an American. That gratitude is a gift I want to share with my children and yours."

Paloma, eleven years old, still treasures her Lady Freedom keychain.

Becoming a Citizen

If you were not born a U.S. citizen, you may become a naturalized citizen if you follow certain rules. These rules include filling out an application, passing a security clearance, and being able to read, write, and speak basic English. New citizens must also show that they have good moral character as well as a knowledge and understanding of U.S. history and government. During the citizenship ceremony, you must be willing to renounce your loyalty to the country you came from and promise to defend the United States from all enemies, foreign and domestic. The oath also requires you to pledge allegiance to the Constitution and laws of the United States.

King George and the American Revolution

King George was the king of England during the American Revolution. He bullied the colonists with unfair taxes. Many colonists decided they didn't want to be ruled by a king anymore. The colonists banded together to denounce "taxation without representation." They boycotted English tea and threw shiploads of tea into the Boston Harbor. This angered King George and caused him to crack down harder on the rebellious colonists. Eventually, the colonists sought independence from England and the Revolutionary War started. After the Americans won the war and their independence, they established the first government in human history that was by and for the people.

Lady Freedom

The American sculptor, Thomas Crawford, designed the classic and graceful bronze statue known as Lady Freedom in 1856 with the approval of Republican President Abraham Lincoln. She is 19.5 feet tall and is dressed as a warrior. She carries a sword and shield in her right hand, and a laurel wreath in her left hand to represent victory over tyranny. Lady Freedom faces east because she is keeping her eye on England to protect America's freedom. The original design of Lady Freedom included a Roman liberty cap, the symbol of freed slaves that was typically used in classical statues depicting freedom and liberty. However, U.S. Secretary of War Jefferson Davis objected to the Roman liberty cap since the statue was erected after slavery was abolished. "Its history," declared Davis, "renders it inappropriate to a people who were born free and should not be enslaved." Thomas Crawford redesigned the helmet with stars and added a crested cap with an eagle's head and bold feathers, resembling a Native American headdress. Lady Freedom stands on a pedestal topped with a globe encircled with the motto E Pluribus Unum (out of many one).

Pocahontas Painting in the Rotunda of U.S. Capitol

Pocahontas was the daughter of the influential Algonkian Chief Powhatan. Her birth name was Amonute, but it is believed she was given the nickname Pocahontas, which means "playful one," because of her happy, inquisitive nature. She must have also been very brave, confident, and intelligent, since historians credit her with playing a crucial role in maintaining good relations between her father's tribe and the Jamestown colonists. In 1613, Pocahontas was kidnapped by an English captain. While in captivity, Pocahontas converted to Christianity, was baptized into the Anglican Church, and given the name Rebecca. In 1614, she married a colonist named John Rolfe. Her dream of friendship and cooperation between nations continues to inspire Americans.

Rosa Parks

Despite being free citizens, black people living in certain parts of America were expected to follow dehumanizing rules such as drinking from "black only" water fountains, attending segregated "black only" schools and restaurants, and sitting in the back of buses. While traveling on buses, black people were also expected to give up their seats for white people. In 1955 in Montgomery, Alabama, a seamstress named Rosa Parks was arrested because she refused to give up her seat to a white man on a bus. Her bravery and peaceful disobedience inspired Americans—black and white—who were thirsty for justice. Her actions ignited the Montgomery bus boycott, which was one of the largest and most successful mass movements against racial segregation in history. Martin Luther King Jr. was one of the organizers of the boycott. This year-long boycott led to the positive changes for freedom and justice in America. Without a question, Rosa Parks changed American history. She is Lady Freedom.